MOVIE THEATER
Storybook

based on *The Railway Series*
by The Reverend W Awdry

Best Friends
Contents

Reader's
Digest
Children's Books®

Pleasantville, New York • Montréal, Québec • Bath, United Kingdom

Edward Strikes Out

DISK 1
1

Edward is a familiar sight to everyone on the Island of Sodor. He has worked on the railway longer than any of the other engines.

One summer morning, Edward arrived at the Docks to pick up a large load of heavy telephone poles. Thomas was busy marveling at the new crane that had just arrived.

"Who is he?" asked Edward.

"I don't know yet," said Thomas. "But it's exciting to have someone new on the Island, isn't it? And he looks strong enough to pick up even Gordon!"

Gordon had overheard Thomas and was not happy about the new crane. Gordon liked being the biggest, strongest engine on Sodor.

"That crane might be big, but he has no engine," chuffed Gordon to Edward. "He can't move unless an engine pulls him."

Edward agreed that just because something was new didn't mean it was better than something that was old. "I don't suppose he can be Really Useful then," said Edward.

Just then Percy came puffing by, boiling over
with excitement about the new crane.

"New-fangled nonsense," huffed Gordon, as
he went away.

Percy was confused. "What's a new funneled
nuisance?" he asked Edward.

"New-fangled nonsense," Edward repeated.
"It's something that's new, but *not* Really
Useful. Just like that silly new crane, Rocky."

Edward puffed away to collect the telephone
poles that had been stacked by Rocky.

"Hello," said the crane. "My name is Rocky.
Can I help you with the poles?"

"My name is Edward," the engine replied. "But I don't need help…new-fangled nonsense," he chuffed.

Edward hurried away so quickly that the telephone poles weren't tied down properly.

"Old things are much more useful than new things," he puffed to himself. Then there was trouble. A signal up ahead changed to red. Edward screeched to a stop, but the telephone poles spilled all over the tracks!

"Bust my buffers!" exclaimed Edward. Harvey, the crane engine, was called to help clean up the mess.

3 Harvey started to lift the heavy poles, but he could only move one at a time. "This is going to take me a very long time," he gasped.

Thomas pulled up, but he couldn't get past the telephone poles.

4 "Why don't we call the new big crane?" Thomas asked Edward. "He'd be much faster at this sort of work."

"No, no," said Edward. "Harvey's doing a fine job. We must be patient."

Suddenly, they heard a voice boom, "Out of my way! Out of my way!" It was Gordon. He was going so fast that he couldn't stop in time.

DISK 2
⑤

CRUNCH! Gordon hit the poles and came off the track!

Edward was horrified. This mess was all his fault!

"I can't lift Gordon," said Harvey. "He's too heavy."

There was only one thing Edward could do.

"I'll go and get Rocky!" he wheeshed, as he raced off.

Edward steamed into the Docks. "Rocky, we need your help!" he whistled. "It's an emergency!"

"I'm happy to help," Rocky replied cheerfully. He was coupled onto Edward. Soon Edward was pulling Rocky along the tracks. People cheered and waved at them.

Edward arrived with Rocky at the junction. Rocky looked at the mess and smiled. "I can fix this!"

With a mighty heave, he quickly set Gordon back on the track.

6

Gordon was surprised. "Thank you, Rocky," he huffed. "Good work."

Then Rocky lifted all the telephone poles back onto Edward's cars. The tracks were clear in no time.

Sir Topham Hatt arrived to check on the situation. He was very happy to see that Rocky had cleared away the mess so quickly.

"Thank you, Rocky," said Sir Topham Hatt. "You've worked hard and have been Really Useful today. Well done!"

Rocky was happy he had been able to help. He smiled as all the engines tooted and cheered.

Edward was sorry he had not been nicer to Rocky. "I'm sorry I called you 'new-fangled nonsense'," he said. "You might be new, but you're also Really Useful. Welcome to the Island of Sodor."

8

Best Friends

Thomas and Percy are the best of friends. They even have a special "Best Friends" whistle. Today they were working a busy day together at the Quarry. They happily tooted their special whistles. "My favorite days are when we work together!" Thomas peeped.

Then Neville arrived with big news. The brass band was arriving at the Docks. Who would be sent to collect them?

"I wish I could do it," Percy chuffed glumly, "but I was never asked."

Thomas wanted his best friend to be happy. "Go to the wash down and you'll be clean and shiny as new," he advised Percy. "Then Sir Topham Hatt will surely ask you." The two engines tooted their Best Friends whistles as Percy happily hurried off.

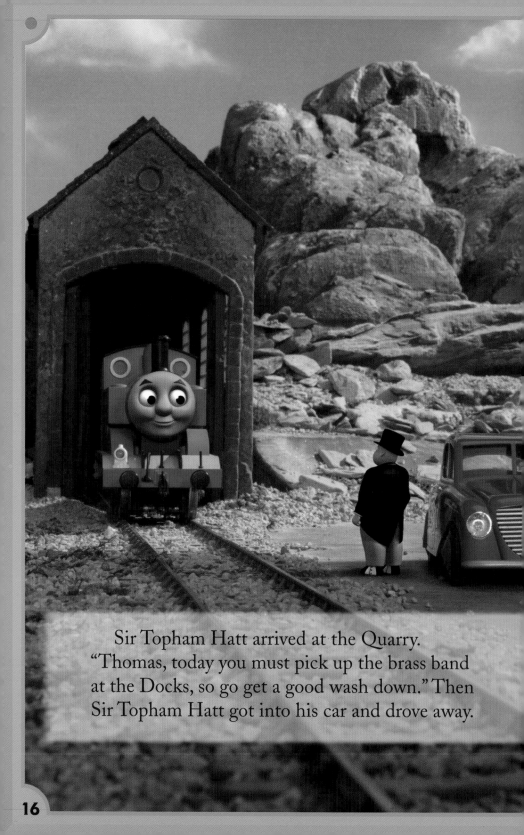

Sir Topham Hatt arrived at the Quarry.
"Thomas, today you must pick up the brass band
at the Docks, so go get a good wash down." Then
Sir Topham Hatt got into his car and drove away.

Next, Percy puffed up from his wash down, shiny as new. "Look, Thomas. Sir Topham Hatt is sure to choose me now!" Percy said. Thomas did not want to hurt his best friend's feelings by telling him he had been asked to pick up the band, so he puffed away.

"Wait, where are you going?" Percy called out.

"I have another job," he peeped as he quickly puffed away. When Percy tooted his Best Friends whistle, Thomas didn't toot back.

Thomas was enjoying his wash down. Then he saw Percy in the distance, so he hid. Now he would have to hurry to collect Annie and Clarabel and meet the brass band on time.

At the Docks, Thomas saw the long line of mail cars. He knew Percy would be coming soon to get them. Thomas tried to hurry the brass band, but the trumpet player had left his horn behind so Thomas had to wait. Percy arrived just as the brass band was boarding Thomas. "Why didn't you tell me, Thomas?" Percy chuffed. Thomas only tooted his Best Friends whistle. Percy didn't toot back.

4 Thomas arrived at Great Waterton with a heavy heart. When Sir Topham Hatt reminded him to return for the brass band, Thomas had an idea. "Sir, what if I pull Percy's mail trucks? Then could Percy take the band?" Sir Topham Hatt agreed! Thomas left Annie and Clarabel and steamed off to find his best friend.

Thomas found Percy waiting at a signal. "I'm sorry I didn't tell you I was picking up the band," Thomas chuffed.

Percy wouldn't look at him. "I'm busy," he puffed. "I have to pull the mail." Then Thomas told him the good news, and Percy beamed from buffer to buffer. "Thank you, Thomas!" Percy cheered.

Percy collected Annie and Clarabel and
arrived just in time! Thomas pulled up right
behind him carrying the mail.

"You are my best friend, Percy," Thomas
reminded him. "From now on, I will always tell
you everything!" Then they each tooted their
Best Friends whistle for all to hear.